Hi! I'm the bus driver. Listen, I've got to leave for a little while, so can you watch things for me until I get back? Thanks. Oh, and remember:

Don't Let the Pigeon Drive the Bus!

words and pictures by mo willems

Hyperion Books for Children / New York

Text and illustrations © 2003
by Mo Willems

This special edition was printed for Kohl's, Inc. (Distribution on behalf of Kohl's Cares, LLC, its wholly owned subsidiary)
by Hyperion Books for Children, an imprint of Buena Vista Books, Inc., New York.

First Edition, April 2003   •   10 9 8 7 6 5 4 3 2 1   •   FAC-025393-22014   •   Printed in China

This book is hand-lettered by Mo Willems, with additional text set in Helvetica Neue LT Pro and Latino Rumba/Monotype.
Library of Congress Cataloging-in-Publication Data on file.
ISBN 978-1-368-08404-8
Visit www.hyperionbooksforchildren.com and www.pigeonpresents.com

This title won a 2004 Caldecott Honor for the
English U.S. Edition published by Hyperion
Books for Children, an imprint of Buena Vista
Books, Inc., in the previous year in 2003.

Kohl's
Style Number 9781368084048
Factory Number 131076
Production Date 01/2022

for cher

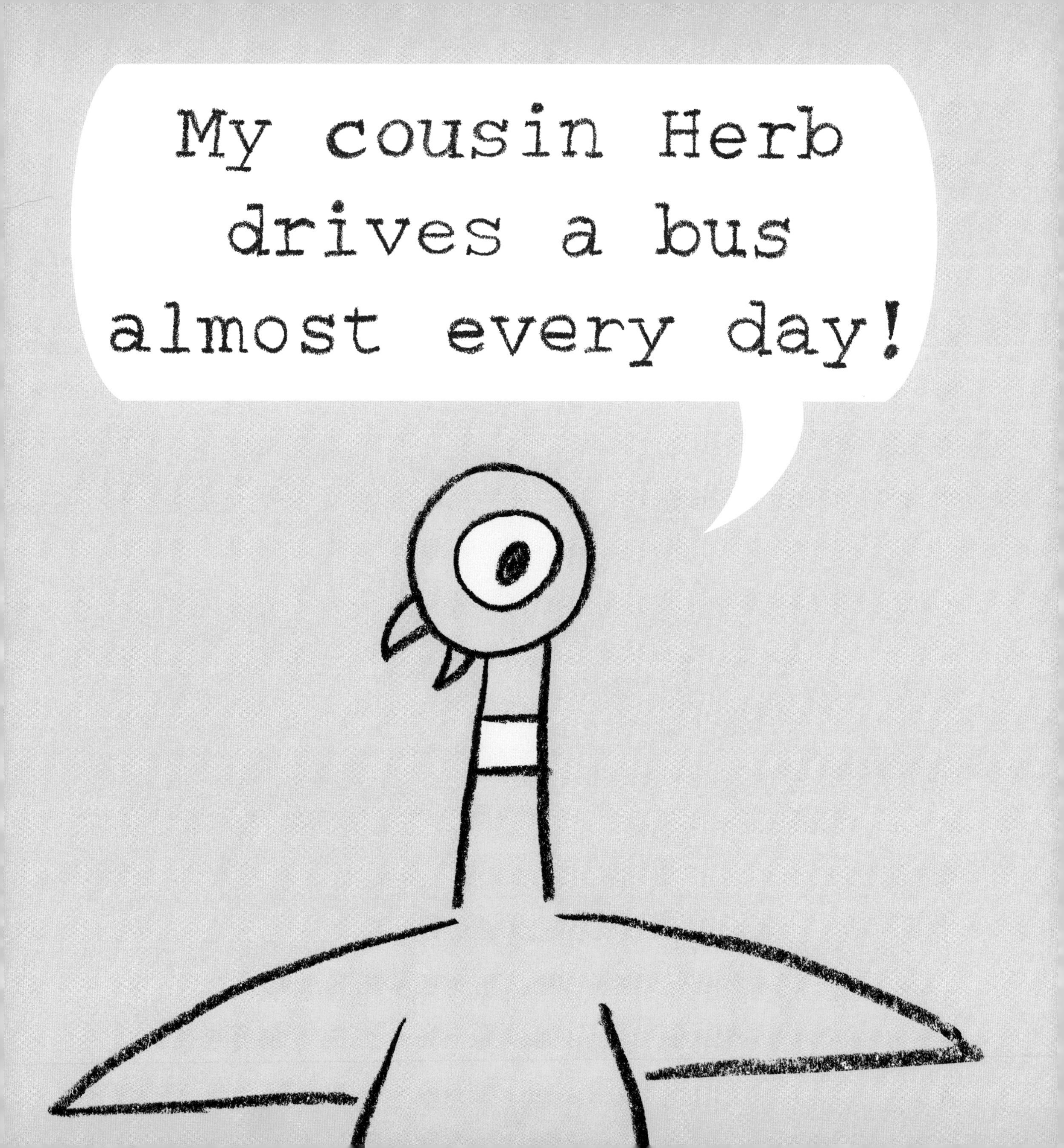
My cousin Herb drives a bus almost every day!

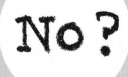

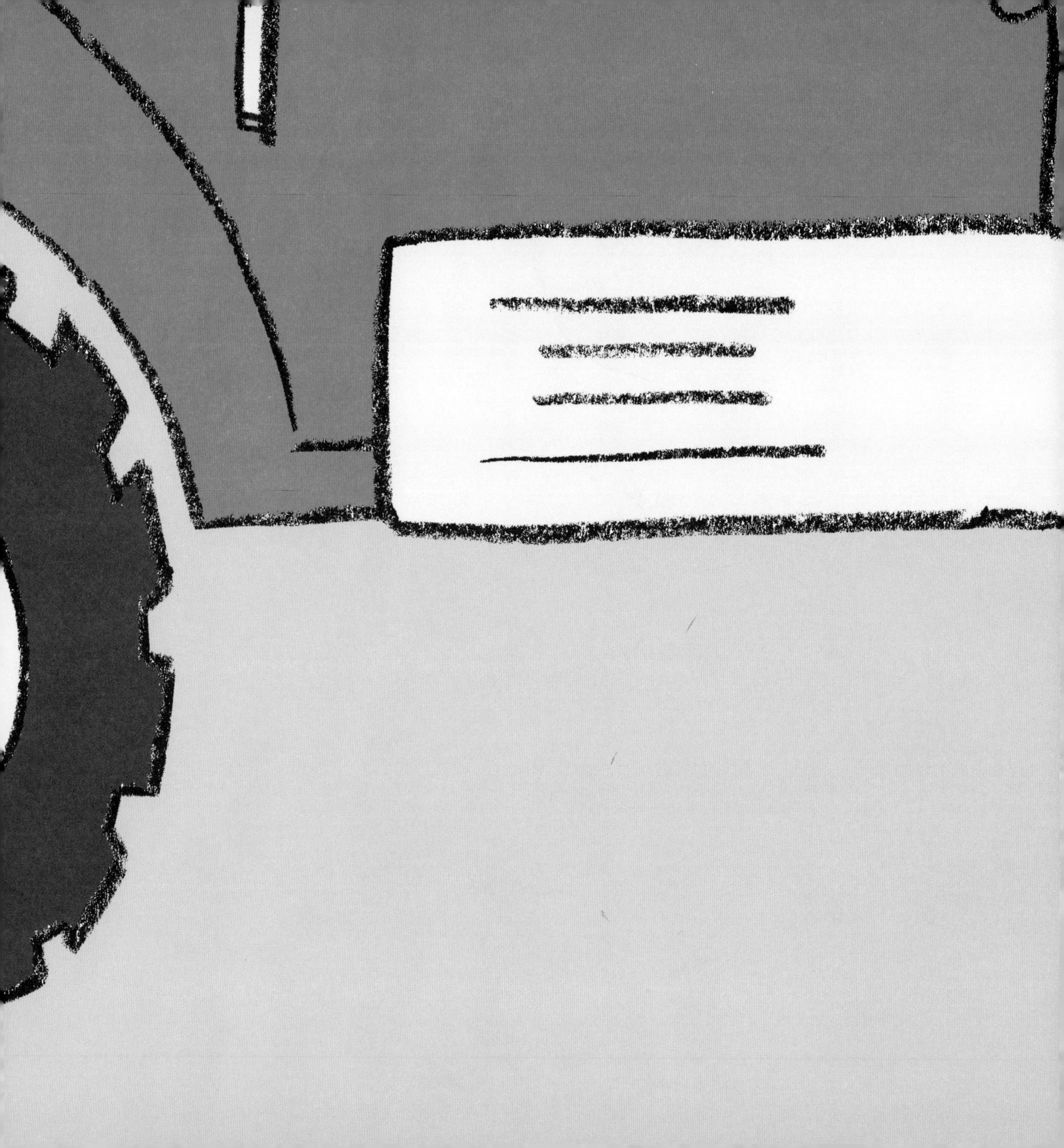